Skimmer

Elaine Jenkins

O&U

Onwards & Upwards

Onwards and Upwards Publishers

3 Radfords Turf, Cranbrook, Exeter,
EX5 7DX, United Kingdom.
www.onwardsandupwards.org

Copyright © Elaine Jenkins 2019

The right of Elaine Jenkins to be identified as the author of this work has been asserted by the author in accordance with the Copyright, Designs and Patents Act 1988.

First edition, published in the United Kingdom by Onwards and Upwards Publishers (2019).

ISBN: 978-1-78815-686-8
Typeface: Sabon LT / KBPlanetEarth
Illustrations: Hannah Stout

Printed in the United Kingdom.

For my three children
and young families everywhere.

Skimmer

1

IT WAS LATE MARCH AND THE AIR WAS STILL chilly. Jobe Evans and his two sisters, Rose and Grace, were on their way home from school. Rose Evans was tall for her eleven years, with long blonde, wavy hair, blue eyes and a beautiful smile. She was a sensible, kind-hearted girl and always good company. Her brother Jobe was ten years old, impulsive, adventurous and passionate, with fiery red hair, a face full of freckles and kind sea-green eyes. Jobe loved to joke around, especially with Grace, which didn't always go down well with her. Grace Evans, the youngest, was eight years old. She looked like an angel, with shiny, light blonde hair, large blue eyes and porcelain skin; but don't be fooled, she was no pushover. In fact, she was the toughest of the three; fearless, stubborn, determined and embarrassingly truthful. Grace just didn't give in to anyone, at least not without a fight.

The children had cut across the beach, which they often did as a shortcut home. Jobe had run ahead. He climbed over the rocks, picking up a few smooth pebbles. He liked the cold smoothness of them, as he rubbed them with his fingers and thumb and turned them over in the palms of his hands. He started to skim the stones on the incoming tide. The girls were chatting about Aimee's birthday party that they had all just been invited to. Aimee was Grace's best friend; they had known each other all their lives. Their mothers were great friends and often met up for a coffee or to go to the local car boot sales together. In the holidays the girls were constantly running in and out of each other's homes and arranging sleepovers.

Suddenly… Jobe stopped. He was staring out across the water. 'Quick, come over here and look.' He was pointing out to sea. 'Oh, hurry up or you'll miss it,' he shouted.

The girls put on some speed and caught him up. 'What is it? Not another monster crab? You know we can't catch it as we haven't brought anything to catch it in,' Rose said, not looking up.

'Shh… Rose, just look out there, towards Hermit Point.'

Hermit Point was an island of rocks and grass, which in low tide you could walk out to, but in high tide you could just see the grassy, rocky top.

'What? What's out there?' said Rose.

'Oh, look, silly, can't you see it?' Jobe was getting a little impatient.

'Well, what am I looking for? I don't see anything.'

'Oh, Rose, look, I see it! I see it!' Grace was getting excited. 'It's between those two big rocks over there,' she said, pointing out to sea.

'Shh, you'll frighten him!' said Jobe.

There was a sudden splash which drew Rose's attention. She stared hard and saw a small fin, then another sighting of a rounded snout, and a black eye looking back at her. A second later it disappeared under the water.

'It's a dolphin! A dolphin!' squealed Grace, jumping up and down.

'Yes! *My* dolphin,' Jobe reminded them.

'What?'

'I found him, didn't I?'

'That's not fair!' cried Grace.

'Don't be silly you two, you can't own a dolphin. He belongs to the sea. Now let's just enjoy him,' said Rose looking straight at Grace with a look that said, *Grace, don't you start.*

'I did see him first!' said Jobe, making his point.

'Yes, we know,' said Rose.

The children watched as the dolphin seemed to ignore them and played in the water quite near to them.

'He's very playful and not very big. I think he's a young one,' explained Rose trying to sound knowledgeable.

Then Jobe did something odd that surprised his sisters. He skimmed one of the pebbles he had in his hand across the water towards the last sighting of the dolphin. Not frightened at all, the dolphin jumped up out of the sea to investigate the bouncing stone.

'Do it again!' cried Grace.

So Jobe skimmed all the smooth pebbles he had collected. The children watched with delight as the dolphin chased them. They watched as he jumped up into the air in beautiful half-moon shapes, and then disappeared into the cold, green sea.

They started guessing where he would appear next. The questions, shouts and laughter between the children were flying back and forth like sea spray as they wondered why he was on his own and wasn't afraid of them.

Now the tide was rapidly moving in. Unless they hurried, the sea would cut them off and they would be stranded.

'Grace, Jobe, we have to go now! The tide is coming in fast and we are going to get soaked!' said Rose, sternly.

The children watched as the dolphin seemed to ignore them and played in the water.

'You go, if you like. I'm staying a bit longer,' said Jobe.

'No, you're not, Jobe, and that's final!' Rose grabbed him by his school jumper and pulled him over to her. 'We're already late anyway, and Mum will start to get worried! You know what she's like,' she continued as she led Jobe towards the harbour.

'OK, I'll come; you can let go now,' said Jobe, as he shrugged away from Rose. 'I wish she would just let us get a phone! Then we could text her to say we're late. The new iPhone looks so cool.'

'I know,' said Rose, 'but I'm sure she'll let us get one when we're a bit older.'

Grace had gone on ahead, hopping from rock to rock, avoiding as much of the sea water as she could.

'Rose,' Jobe said, 'it would be sad if we didn't see him again – the dolphin, I mean. I really liked him.'

'Me too, but we have had a great afternoon with him, and we know he's out there now. Let's come back to-morrow and see if we can find him again.'

By now they had caught up with Grace who had been listening to their conversation. 'Yes, let's come here tomorrow. This is the best thing that's happened today. Well... this and getting Aimee's birthday invite.'

For a change, Grace knew exactly what she was going to give Aimee this year for her ninth birthday. Aunty Ali's sheepdog, Molly, had given birth to puppies six weeks ago. Aunty Ali had put aside one little girl pup that Grace had chosen. Keeping it a secret from Aimee was one of the hardest things Grace had ever done, as they shared just about everything, being best friends.

They were almost at the slipway by the fishermen's harbour and had just beaten the tide as it soaked the sand behind them.

'Come on! Let's run, or Mum's going to be cross,' shouted Rose.

'Do we have to tell Mum and Dad about the dolphin? Can it be our secret?' said Jobe.

'I don't see why not,' said Rose.

'Not *another* secret I can't tell Aimee about!' Grace protested.

'Well, not yet, anyway,' smiled Rose.

'That's *two* things I can't talk to Aimee about now, and they're the most exciting things I know. It's going to be so-o-o-o hard, especially at school,' Grace moaned. She didn't like keeping secrets.

When the children arrived home, their Mum stood at the doorway, her arms folded with *that* look on her face. 'Well, where have you three been?' Without waiting for an answer, she went on, 'You should have been back ages ago.'

'Yes, Mum, sorry! We were having so much fun at the beach,' Grace blurted out.

Both Rose and Jobe flashed Grace a look that said *be quiet!*

Luckily, Mum didn't notice, and continued. 'Rose and you two little ones...' (Jobe hated being called that; it made him feel like a baby, and he wasn't.) '...that's all very well, but it is high tide this week and you all know the rules: no playing on the beach when it's high tide; not without an adult. Now, come on, hang your coats up and get on with your homework; it's nearly supper time.'

'Mum, can I use the laptop? I've got some research to do for a project,' asked Rose.

'That's fine. Grace, you come into the kitchen with me and we will do your reading,' said Mum walking ahead.

The children smiled at each other. *That was close;* their secret was still safe.

2

THE NEXT DAY AS THE CHILDREN SET OFF FOR school, they talked of nothing else but the young dolphin out at Hermit Point and what to wear for Aimee's birthday party. Well, the girls did... School passed slowly, but at last, the final bell went. Rose went in search of Jobe and Grace, but she needn't have as they were already waiting by the school gates.

'All day I've been waiting for this,' said Grace. 'Hurry up!' She was so desperate to talk to someone about their secret dolphin, even if it was only her brother and sister. It made her impatient. 'Come on, Rose, let's go,' she shouted.

Once on the beach, they each collected a handful of smooth pebbles for skimming with. They clambered over the rocks, trying not to slip into the rock pools, which wasn't easy as the rocks were covered in slimy, wet seaweed. They were heading out to Hermit Point, ignoring their mother's warning about *not* playing on the beach when the tide was high. Grace was leading the way. She started to throw her pebbles.

'Not like that, Grace,' laughed Jobe. 'Throw it at a sideways angle, just above the water – like this.' He showed her as he spoke.

She had another go.

'Not like that, Grace,' laughed Jobe.

'That's a bit better; remember it's a sideways sort of throw as if you want the stone to stroke the top of the water.'

'Stroke, hey?' said Grace, getting a little better with each attempt, although she did not find it easy.

'Well done, that's a bit better,' encouraged Rose.

'Yeah, but you need to keep practising,' laughed Jobe.

The three children practised together, improving their technique and competing against each other for the greatest number of skims. Of course, Jobe was the one to beat. Then play was interrupted as a tail splash and a small fin appeared above the water.

This time it was Rose who spotted him first. 'Look! He's back! *Oh, wow!* Look at him go; he's so fast and smooth in the water.'

'He's beautiful!' squealed Grace with delight. 'I hoped he would come back.'

Jobe tried to get closer, but he slipped on a slippery seaweed rock and landed in a shallow rock pool, soaking his shoes, socks and the bottom half of his trousers, and making his sisters laugh.

'Serves you right for showing off,' laughed Grace. 'You always try to be better than us.'

The dolphin seemed to be having as much fun as the children. He was quite a show-off. He jumped out of the water and did great tail splashes as he slid back in, then he would dive deep into the cold, green sea. All would go quiet for a second or two, and then out he'd jump, appearing in a different spot. The children would guess where he would next appear and then boast about how clever they were when one of them got it right. Time flew by as they played, until Rose's shoes started to get wet from the tide that had silently surrounded them.

'Oh no! We have to go; the tide's coming in fast! We'll have to swim for it, if we don't leave now.' Rose sounded a little scared.

Grace and Jobe listened this time. The three of them retreated back over the rocks, criss-crossing them as quickly as they could, turning it into a game.

'That was a bit close,' laughed Jobe.

'Yes, a bit *too* close!' agreed Rose.

Walking home, Grace said, 'He needs a name. Our dolphin needs a name.'

While the girls were still thinking, Jobe blurted out, 'I like Nemo… or what about Steve?'

Jobe always liked to lead and be the first at everything, even if he hadn't thought things through.

'Jobe, I don't think that really suits him, and we don't know if he is a male or female dolphin.' Rose spoke kindly, not wanting to upset her brother.

There was a long pause.

'Well, I like the name Skimmer,' Grace chipped in. 'I think we should call him that. He comes when we skim stones. It suits him, and it doesn't matter if he's a girl or boy, he could still be called Skimmer,' she continued in her matter-of-fact way.

Rose looked at Jobe and then they both looked at Grace.

'Grace, that's a great name,' said Jobe, a bit surprised at himself. He was, after all, agreeing with his sister on a very important decision that he hadn't made.

'Grace, I love it too! *Skimmer,'* Rose smiled.

On the rare occasion when Grace blurted out the name Skimmer at school, no one knew what she was talking about. The next couple of days they walked home from school along the beach, hoping to see and play with him.

3

AS THE DAYS ROLLED BY, THE BEACH BECAME A regular detour on the way home as they went to see Skimmer. He seemed to wait for them. He would be nowhere in sight until he saw the stones bounce and jump across the water. Then he would miraculously appear as if he was just waiting for them.

'If we had a camera we could take some great shots of Skimmer. I've got some pocket money saved up, so tonight I will see how much I have. Hopefully it will be enough for a waterproof camera – you know, the disposable kind? If it is, we can go and buy one in the chemist after school tomorrow.'

'Great idea, Rose. You know I would help towards it if I had any money,' said Jobe, turning his trouser pockets inside out and showing the lining of his trousers, then shrugging his shoulders as if to say, *sorry, I can't help.*

'I'll help out, Rose, if you don't have enough money,' added Grace. Grace was reluctant to spend her money on anything unless absolutely necessary, but for this she would dip into her savings.

———————————

When they reached home, Mum was in the kitchen taking the last tray of scones out of the oven. The children

*Skimmer would be nowhere in sight
until he saw the stones bounce.*

dropped their school bags on the floor, then took their coats off and hung them up.

Hello, you three! How was school?'

'Yeah, not too bad. Mmm… smells great, Mum! Can I have one?' asked Jobe as he reached for the plate of hot scones on the table.

'Yes, Jobe, but be careful, they're hot. You have just seen me take them out of the oven.'

Grace and Rose also tucked in, each taking a hot scone and spreading it thickly with butter, which quickly melted into the scone. Then they added a large dollop of strawberry jam on top and washed it all down with a cold glass of milk. After they had eaten two each, they settled down to do their homework. When that was finished, Rose went upstairs, while Jobe and Grace watched TV. Rose emptied her piggy bank onto her bed and counted out her savings. To her surprise, she had more money than she thought. Rose took out ten pounds, put it to one side and put the rest back into her piggy bank. With the ten pounds, all in coins, she went downstairs and quietly put it into a zipped pocket of her school bag. 'Now I am ready for after school tomorrow,' she said to herself.

———————

The next day, when classes were finished, Grace, Jobe and Rose walked down to Havenston High Street, missing the beach completely. As they stepped inside the chemist's door, the bell above the door rang out announcing a customer.

Mr. Singh popped his head up from behind the counter. 'Can I help you?' he smiled.

'Yes please, we need a disposable camera and it needs to be waterproof.'

Rose unzipped the pocket of her school bag and reached for her coins.

'Over there, between the toothpaste and the sunscreen,' Mr. Singh said, pointing to the aisle behind them.

Jobe shot round and found them. There were five different types to choose from. Only three were under ten pounds and only one was waterproof. 'Well, that's easy; we will take this one.' He reached up for the blue plastic one at £9.99 and took it off the shelf, then took it over to the counter where Mr. Singh was waiting.

Rose handed the carefully counted money over to Mr. Singh. 'That was a good guess, wasn't it?' she said, smiling at Mr. Singh.

With the camera safely tucked into her school bag, the three of them left the chemist and walked home.

It was now only two days before Aimee's birthday. Grace was beside herself with excitement and she couldn't stop talking of different ways she could wrap up the puppy for Aimee.

'Grace, you are funny! Perhaps we should put the puppy in a box with holes in and tie a big red bow round the box, then give it to Aimee like that?' said Mum.

'No, Mum, that's boring! It's Friday tomorrow, Mum; can we go to Aunty Ali's straight after school and pick up the puppy? Then we will be ready for the party on Saturday morning.'

'We'll go tomorrow once your homework is finished so that's out of the way,' said Mum. 'I'll make an early supper and then we will go to Aunty Ali's to collect the puppy. We'll take Laddie with us. He could do with a run around as I won't have time to walk him tomorrow.'

'Great!' exclaimed Grace.

The next day was amazing. Aimee was a class favourite; everyone liked her. She was kind, easy-going and very bright. The whole class had been invited to her party because Aimee had persuaded her mum that it wasn't fair for only half the class to come when they all wanted to. They sang "Happy Birthday" in school and a few of the children who couldn't make the party brought in little gifts. Aimee handed these to her teacher, still wrapped up so she could take them home and open them at her party. This, Grace couldn't understand. She would have opened them straight away to see what she had been given.

Once home, they changed out of their school uniforms, brought them down to be washed and then got on with their homework. It was easy for Grace; she had a chapter to read and then had to colour in King Henry VIII. Jobe had spellings to learn, which he never found easy, and a page of maths to finish off. Rose had her maths times tables to go over for a test on Monday. Once all that was done, Mum served up scrambled eggs on toast.

After tea they jumped into the car with Laddie the dog and drove to Aunty Ali's. It wasn't far. Aunty Ali lived on the outskirts of town surrounded by fields and woodland. It was great for Molly, Aunty Ali's sheepdog, who loved to be outside running around playing and rounding up the neighbours' hens. It was always good to see Aunty Ali. She was great fun and she made them laugh, even when she was telling them off, which she often did. She was taller than Mum, with thick, dark, shiny hair, smiley hazel-green eyes and big feet.

Once they arrived, Aunty Ali handed a beautiful black and white fluffy puppy to Grace. As the puppy licked her face and wriggled in her arms, Grace buried her face into the warm, soft fur breathing in the sweet puppy smell. Laddie had found Molly and they were playing outside, barking and chasing each other round in circles.

In the kitchen Aunty Ali had made her wonderful chocolate cake and a cheesecake which the children loved. She could cook anything, especially cakes. So, while Jobe and Rose were waiting for their turn to hold the puppy, they tucked into Aunty Ali's cakes.

They each had a large slice of both; it would have been rude not to and they had only had a light supper so there was still plenty of room in their tummies. Rose and Jobe finally got their chance to greet and meet Aimee's little puppy. She was gorgeous, very friendly and loved being cuddled, which was just as well. The evening slipped by and a sort of calm settled in Aunty Ali's house.

It was now getting late. Grace had curled up with the puppy on the sofa and both had fallen asleep. Rose and Jobe had an armchair each, with full, happy tummies, watching TV.

'Oh Ali, look at them,' whispered Mum. 'I had better get the children home, then settle this little pup. It's going to be a big day tomorrow. Aimee is going to be over the moon when she sees the puppy; she has always wanted one. As usual, the cakes were delicious.' She gave her sister a kiss.

Mum picked up Grace, Rose picked up the puppy and Jobe grabbed hold of Laddie, who still wanted to play.

'Thanks, Aunty Ali,' yawned Rose. 'It's been great fun and you still make the best cheesecake in the world.'

'Yup, thanks Aunty Ali.' Jobe went over and gave her a hug. 'And the best chocolate cake.'

He loved Aunty Ali – even if she told him off more often than the girls (which he normally deserved).

4

THE NEXT DAY WAS SATURDAY AND GRACE WAS up first. She jumped out of bed and ran into the kitchen to check on Laddie. Well, actually, to see and check on Aimee's puppy.

Laddie was such a kind old dog and was taking care of the mischievous little puppy. When he saw the door open and Grace appear, he wagged his tail and came straight over to greet her, giving her a nudge and trying to lick her face.

'Hi, Laddie, did you sleep well?' Grace said quietly, not wanting to wake the sleeping puppy or the rest of the household. She found the puppy in Laddie's bed, not in the prepared cardboard box that Mum had left her in. 'Poor Laddie! You are such a good boy!' said Grace thoughtfully. 'You've even given up your bed for the puppy.' She gave him a cuddle and a kiss.

After greeting Laddie, Grace went over to pick up the sleeping floppy, fluffy puppy. 'Oh, I wish you were mine,' she said as she kissed the waking puppy. 'Aimee's going to love you so much. You are going to a good home,' she continued, burying her face in the warm, soft fur. 'You are the best present ever.'

There were stirrings in the house now. The loo flushed and Dad coughed, and before long everyone was down having breakfast, including Laddie and the puppy. After breakfast was cleared away and a few house chores were done, Mum and the children dressed ready for Aimee's party. Dad had decided to stay at home, walk Laddie and get some shopping in, then watch the rugby match on TV. Grace wore her favourite yellow and white cotton dress with a blue cardigan that Aunty Ali had made for her last Christmas. Jobe had on his best jeans and new shirt. Rose wore a dress of printed cherries on a turquoise background with her cardigan that Aunty Ali had also knitted for her. Mum always made an effort. She wore a pretty shirt with her favourite cashmere wrap over her jeans. She also gave Grace and Rose a squirt of her perfume. Grace wanted to put a pink bow on the puppy, but the puppy was having none of it. She kept pulling it off to play with, which made the ribbon look very tatty. So after trying several times, the puppy won and the pink bow stayed home.

The party was from noon to 3.00pm, though the Evans family were going early to help Aimee's mum to set up a few of the last minute things. Mum and Aimee's mum had been friends since primary school and were as close as sisters.

When they arrived at Aimee's, Grace put the puppy under her cardigan to try to hide her from Aimee for as long as possible. It made her laugh as the puppy wriggled around a lot.

Aimee answered the door looking lovely with her brown hair back from her face in plaits with red bows tied to the ends and wearing a very pretty red dress. She rushed in excitement to give Grace a big hug, and before Grace

*Grace put the puppy under her cardigan
to try to hide her from Aimee.*

could stop her, she had squashed the puppy, which let out a yelp. 'Oh, what's that?' Aimee cried in surprise.

'Your birthday present.'

Then a fluffy, black and white head popped out through an undone button hole.

'Oh, is she mine? Have you really brought her for me?' cried Aimee.

'Yes, silly, it's your birthday present. Aunty Ali's dog, Molly, had pups and I chose her for you. I know how much you like Laddie, and Mum asked your mum if it would be OK. It's been the hardest secret to keep from you,' she said, untangling the puppy from her cardigan and handing her over to Aimee.

It was love at first sight; the puppy licked Aimee all over her face. Aimee ran inside to show her mum. Her mum waved everyone in, and laughter and chatter quickly filled the house; it took a good while to settle everybody down. Jobe and Rose were given the jobs of blowing up the balloons and tying them around the house, on the gate, front door and in the garden; Mum helped Aimee's mum with the finishing touches to Aimee's beautiful pink and white cake; and Aimee and Grace played outside with the puppy.

Before long the party was in full swing. The house was full of children, noise, screams, laughter, shouting, music and lots of wrapping paper. Aimee kept her best present with her in her arms and only handed her over when she had to, like when she blew the candles out and made a wish. Then Aimee's mum finally got to hold her, though not for long. The party flew by, games were played, prizes won, yummy food eaten and the odd drink spilt. Bits of cake were squashed into the carpet, the presents were half-opened and there was wrapping paper all over the place. None of that mattered though; happiness was here.

Once the last child – with party bag – had gone, Rose, Jobe and Grace helped tidy up. It didn't take long. They filled a black bag with rubbish from inside the house and another one in the garden. Aimee's mum cut a wedge of birthday cake for the children to take home with them as well as their party bags. Aimee and her mum waved them goodbye until the Evans family were out of sight.

'What a day! Mum, that was the best birthday ever. Thank you so much,' Aimee said, giving her mum a hug as they closed the door behind them.

The next day was a sunny Sunday. As usual, the Evans family went to church. Grace was looking out for Aimee and she scanned the congregation, eventually finding her. Aimee had saved her a seat and was patting it.

'Mum, can I go and sit with Aimee please?'

'Yes, you can, but no talking.' Mum knew that was wishful thinking.

Aimee's mum nodded a greeting to Grace's parents. Jobe had found seats near the back.

Aimee and Grace worked out that they could do their talking when everyone was singing. So that's what they did most of the time. Today the sermon was about taking our troubles to Jesus and not just doing whatever we felt like doing.

After the service, teas and coffees were served with a selection of biscuits, though you had to be quick to get the chocolate ones. The children would run free until the parents had finished chatting and catching up with each other. It was, in some cases, the only time of the week that they could meet up, as everyone had such busy lives. It was also a good way to meet and welcome newcomers to the church. Church was an important part of village life. Not that everyone went – they didn't – but it was a great source of friendship and help. Most of the week the church had something on. It ran a mothers and toddlers coffee morning on Mondays, and prayer and communion on Wednesday mornings followed by a cup of tea and a piece of cake, a real favourite with the elderly. There were flower-arranging classes, dance classes in the evening for those who wanted to get and stay fit, as well as after-school ballet lessons for the under-ten-year-olds. There was also a Bible study on Friday mornings and the local youth club on Friday nights. So the church building was quite a central part of village life.

Aimee still hadn't decided on a name for her puppy, but they were now down to two: Rosie or Bella. She ran the names past Grace, who immediately preferred Bella. Aimee said that she would talk to her mum again and let her know which one she had chosen tomorrow before school started.

By now it was time for everyone to go home for their lunch and enjoy the rest of their Sunday.

5

THE NEXT DAY, WHEN GRACE SAW AIMEE AT THE school gates, she ran over to her.

'Well, what have you decided to call her?'

Aimee smiled. 'Bella!' she declared.

'I knew you would. Did you know it means "beautiful"? I looked it up,' said Grace as the two girls crossed the playground and walked into class together.

School went quickly. It wasn't long before it was home time as the final bell rang out.

After school Jobe and his sisters headed for the beach. A race started between Jobe and Grace (they were both very competitive). They were running towards Hermit Point to see Skimmer and were jumping rocks and rock pools of various sizes to get there first. Rose was quietly standing by one of the largest rock pools looking at some shrimps swimming around and a small green-grey crab that had crawled out from some rubbery brown seaweed. She had reached into her school bag for her camera and was winding it forward, preparing to take the first photo. That's when she heard Grace scream!

Grace had been racing Jobe over the rock pools and she had slipped on some seaweed. She had fallen sideways into a large rock pool. Not thinking, Rose looked up and pressed the button on her camera and caught Grace in mid-fall. *Splash!* Water everywhere! Grace was totally drenched from head to toe and she just sat there in the rock pool, soaked! Jobe was bent over double, laughing. Rose went to stretch out her hand to help a dripping, clambering Grace get up, but she too was laughing so much that her strength had gone.

'It's not funny! Look at me; I'm soaked. Stop laughing, it's not funny!' Grace shouted, getting angrier and angrier. Up she got, then turned away from her brother and sister and headed home, clearly very upset.

'OK! OK! Sorry! Grace, wait! I'm sorry; are you alright?' called Rose.

'Yeah, Grace, wait for us,' Jobe shouted, still laughing as he ran to catch the girls up.

'Come on, Grace, don't be like that. It *was* funny.'

'Funny? What's funny about it? I'm cold and soaked and I hurt my bum.' Grace wiped away an angry tear.

There was a short pause.

'What's Mum going to say when she sees me like this? She's going to kill me. You know we're not meant to be on the beach. I bet I'll lose my pocket money and have to go to bed early.'

'We'll think of something, Grace,' said Rose, taking off her coat. 'Here, this will warm you up.'

'What if she doesn't let me play on the Wii anymore!'

Jobe took Grace's wet school bag and carried it for her, while Rose helped a cold, squelchy Grace off the beach.

When they reached home, Rose and Jobe distracted their mum by keeping her talking in the kitchen so Grace could dart upstairs to change into some dry clothes and hang the wet ones over the radiator in her bedroom.

*'It's not funny! Look at me; I'm soaked.
Stop laughing, it's not funny!' Grace shouted,
getting angrier and angrier.*

For the rest of the week, the children did not visit the beach to see Skimmer, nor did they tell their parents what had happened on Monday after school. But on Sunday evening, while everyone was eating supper at the dinner table, Dad said, 'Let's take a picnic over to Hermit Point next Saturday. We'll take *Miss Daisy* and we might do a spot of fishing; what do you think?'

'What a lovely idea!' said Mum. 'I haven't been on *Miss Daisy* for ages and it will be good to sail her out there if the weather's fine.'

The three children looked at each other nervously.

'Mmm, good idea,' they murmured, trying to sound positive and then changing the subject quickly. 'Can I use your nail varnish and paint Grace's and my nails, as it's the weekend?'

'Yes, of course, love,' replied Mum as she got up to clear the plates from the table.

6

WHEN THE CHILDREN WALKED TO SCHOOL THE next day, Rose said out loud what everyone was thinking. 'We are going to have to tell Mum and Dad about Skimmer.'

'Do we *have* to?' moaned Jobe.

'Yes, I think we do. They will find out anyway and maybe they will be able to help him out.'

The children walked on in silence for a while.

Then Rose continued, 'We've kept Skimmer a secret for this long; it's only a matter of time before someone else sees him and tries to catch him. We'll tell them tonight at supper time.'

Her brother and sister nodded in agreement.

As they reached school and were pairing off to go into their own classrooms, they saw Billy Boot, who was drinking from the water fountain outside his classroom. On seeing Jobe and Rose, he filled his mouth with water and waited till Jobe was walking past. Then he popped his cheeks with his hands, spitting water all over the back of Jobe's coat and school bag.

'Billy!' shouted Rose, wiping Jobe's coat with a tissue from her pocket, while at the same time holding Jobe back from hitting Billy.

*He popped his cheeks with his hands,
spitting water all over the back of
Jobe's coat and school bag.*

Billy had never liked Jobe, but it had got worse since his mother had died. He had picked on him all through school. He would tease him about his red hair, his freckles, anything that would come to mind. Billy was tall for his age, well built, with a turned-up nose and brown eyes, but not a happy or kind boy. He was the sort of boy that would bump into you in the corridor on purpose, turning to hit you with his rucksack, then apologise, pretending it was an accident, so that he wouldn't get into trouble. Billy was not a popular boy; he had a cruel streak in him and because of his size, you didn't mess with him. He was in Rose's class and she didn't like him either, though some of the children felt sorry for him because he was only seven years old when his mother had died. He was a lonely, angry boy.

When he played team games and his side was losing, out would come the dirty tactics and someone usually got hurt (even if the teachers were paying attention). He wasn't very good at taking turns or sharing either. He was an only child and always wanted his own way. He thought kindness was for wimps. Billy was set on being the toughest kid in the school, even if it meant he had no real friends except those who were frightened of him and a few who found his meanness funny.

Today Jobe tried hard to ignore Billy. He had more important things on his mind, but Billy wasn't easy to ignore. Without Rose's help, it would have been impossible. Rose made sure that she, Imogen and Felicity, her best friends, stayed near to Jobe during playtime so she could keep an eye on both boys. She knew her brother and she knew Billy. Billy was itching for a fight and Jobe could only be pushed so far before he would explode. The last thing she wanted was to have to wait after school because

Jobe had received a detention for fighting. Finally, school finished with no fighting and no detentions for either boy. *Yes-s-s! Result!*

———————

That evening, Mum had cooked spaghetti bolognese with grated cheese and herb-filled garlic bread (Grace's favourite). Normally the house would be buzzing with voices overlapping each other trying to be heard, but not tonight. No one had much to say.

'OK, what's wrong, you three? What's happened?' said Dad, finishing his meal.

There was an awkward silence. Jobe kicked Rose under the table.

'Aww!' said Rose rubbing her leg. 'Well, there is something we want to talk to you about.'

Before she could continue, Grace blurted out, 'We will only tell you if you promise not to catch him and kill him.'

'Grace, darling, what is it?' Mum sounded concerned. She and Dad looked at each other. 'We can't promise anything until we know what it is, but we can promise we will do what we think is best.'

Grace, Jobe and Rose told them everything: how they had first seen Skimmer, where they had found him, about his name and the skimming stones game they had played with him, and why they were sometimes late back after school. They talked for ages about how friendly he was.

Dad sat in silence the whole time.

Then he spoke. 'You need to show me where you found him. If the fishermen spot him they might catch him, or anyone else could for that matter. I don't know how we are going to stop that from happening.'

'They can't catch him… He trusts us, and we have to keep him safe. He's done nothing wrong.' Rose was close to tears.

'That's why we've kept him a secret!' shouted Grace.

'Grace, we are fishermen. That's what we do. We catch fish – and he could easily get caught up in our nets,' said Dad softly.

'Skimmer is *not* a fish! He's a dolphin and not just any dolphin; he's *our* dolphin.'

By now both girls were crying. Jobe started arguing with his dad.

'Calm down; let's all calm down,' said Mum. 'We can't do anything by shouting at each other. This won't resolve the matter.' She leaned over and gave Grace a kiss on her head and Rose a hug. Then she started to clear the table.

Rose got up and helped tidy the dishes away with her mother. Grace joined them in the kitchen where Mum made a tray of hot chocolate and took it into the lounge where Dad and Jobe were still in a heated debate about Skimmer.

'OK, you two, there is nothing we can do tonight. Come on, everyone, here's a mug of hot chocolate.' It was starting to get late. 'Drink up, then off to bed. I'll be up to tuck you in and say your prayers.'

On this night they all had something to pray about – his name was Skimmer.

7

TUESDAY WAS A SLOW DAY FOR THE CHILDREN and they felt worried and a bit down, thinking of what could happen to Skimmer. They didn't go home along the beach but took the route through town, still talking about the argument the night before.

Wednesday was worse. Billy spent most of his lunchtime picking on Jobe, calling him names whenever he saw him: 'Rust Bucket!' 'Ginger Nut!' 'Freckle Face! And so it went on.

Jobe did his best to ignore Billy. A few of his friends called him over to play football with them, but Billy wasn't going to give up so easily. Whenever Billy could, he would jump into the game and tackle Jobe, either tripping him or shoving him.

Jobe had had enough! He pushed Billy back – hard. 'Billy, I am not scared of you; you are nothing but a bully. No wonder you don't have any friends. You can't play football or any games for that matter; you are just a fat, sad idiot.' Then he turned and walked off, leaving the game, while Billy stood there with an embarrassed look on his face.

Jobe had never given Billy a real dressing down before. He had on occasions used his fists but this time it was his mouth that had done the damage. It was rude and cruel, but he felt pleased with himself. Normally, when it got too

Jobe had had enough!

much, he would punch Billy. He was one of the only boys in the school who would. This time he had managed to control his fists, but not his mouth. 'That's some progress,' Jobe thought.

Some of Jobe's friends had followed him off the pitch. 'Hey, Jobe! Look, there's four of us. Let's just beat him up. None of us can stand him and maybe he'll stop bullying you.'

'Nice idea, Josh, but I don't think that's going to work. He'll just hate us – well, *me* – even more. Plus, Mrs. Featherspoon will be on us like a ton of bricks! Knowing my luck, I will get suspended.'

'Jobe, he deserves a taste of his own medicine; walking away doesn't make any difference. He just thinks he can get away with it all the time and he pretty much does. I just want to knock him out!'

'No, there has to be another way, Josh. Jobe's right,' said Boaz.

'What then? How do you beat your enemy without punching him? God only knows!'

'Yeah, but I wish he would tell me, and soon!' said Jobe.

The boys laughed and picked up the ball to start a new game. Minutes later, the bell went for end of lunch and back to class.

At the end of the day, Jobe and Grace went out and waited by the school gates for Rose. She was out late. Billy was shouting names at her from behind. Rose knew it was pointless arguing with him so had just walked off. Out in the playground watching all this was Mrs. Featherspoon, the school headmistress. She heard Billy shouting names at Rose and in a stern voice called him over.

'Oops... Caught red-handed!' whispered Rose, and she couldn't help herself as a smile spread over her face.

Billy was escorted back into school by Mrs. Featherspoon.

The next day it was Billy with a smile on his face, his hands in his pockets, leaning against the monkey bars in the playground. Rose looked straight at him. She felt uneasy.

'Come on, Jobe, just ignore him.'

Billy was close – now *too* close – and as quick as a flash, he tugged at Jobe's P.E. bag. Off it slipped into Billy's hand and he ran off with it.

'Oh, for goodness' sake!' cried Rose.

Jobe started to chase him. This was just what Billy wanted. He dodged and weaved his way through other children. Jobe wasn't going to give up. Rose and Grace also tried to catch Billy but couldn't hold onto him long enough to get the bag back.

The bell went for class to start and the children started to go into their classrooms. Billy still had Jobe's P.E. bag, but by now he was getting breathless and slowing down, so it would be just a matter of time before Jobe caught up with him.

'Watch out, Billy,' shouted Frank.

Jobe was now really angry, and Rose knew a fight would break out this time. 'Grace, you go into class now. I will help Jobe,' she said.

Soon there were only a few stragglers left outside with Billy, Jobe and Rose.

'I'm bored of this game!' said a breathless Billy. Taking Jobe's bag off his back and rolling it up into a ball shape, he threw it onto the classroom roof. 'Good shot!' he shouted to himself as he ran into class.

'You stupid idiot, now look what you've done! Wait till I get hold of you,' Jobe shouted after him. 'How am I going to do games now?'

Just then the caretaker came round the corner after hearing Jobe's voice. 'What's all this noise? Shouldn't you two be in class now?' He looked up to where the children were looking and saw Jobe's P.E. bag lying there. 'That's detention for you, Jobe. I will talk to Mrs. Featherspoon about this. This is not the first time you have done this, is it? Now, get into class. I'll have to bring the ladder round to get it down.'

'It wasn't me!' Jobe argued.

'No, Jobe, it never is, is it?'

'That's not fair!' Jobe protested. 'It *wasn't* me. Why don't you believe me?'

'Well, it wasn't Rose, was it? And you two are the only ones out here.'

'Come on, Jobe, let's go,' said Rose, taking her brother gently by the arm.

Just when they thought the day couldn't get any worse, it did.

First break came and went, and Billy wasn't to be seen. He had somehow kept out of Jobe's way, which was just as well. Rose had run out to talk to Jobe about not making matters worse and told him that she and Grace would speak to Mrs. Featherspoon at lunch break so hopefully he wouldn't get a detention. But if he did, they would wait for him after school. Felicity needed the loo, so she was late joining Rose in the playground. She saw Billy hanging around the cloakroom. He seemed to be playing with and opening something. At the time, Felicity didn't give it much thought, though she did notice that he was by the girls' coats and lunchboxes, not where the boys should have been. Soon break was over; it was back into class.

Jobe had to sit in isolation with a teacher while games went on. This made him very cross and moody, but there wasn't much he could do. It was his word against the caretaker's; he knew Billy wouldn't own up. This felt so unfair.

Then the lunch bell went. The children charged into the cloakroom to grab their lunchboxes and headed outside to find and save a seat on the benches for themselves and their friends. Rose was no different; she reached for her lunchbox and looked for Felicity and Imogen. She then opened her lunchbox and immediately screamed and dropped it on the floor.

Rose's teacher made her way towards her. 'What's the matter Rose?'

Rose was crying. 'Look!' she said, pointing down to her open lunchbox.

Everyone looked. Rose's lunch was... *moving*. Well, you could say it was wriggling. Her sandwiches, fruit and carton of juice were covered in maggots! There were so many that they had started to climb out of the lunchbox and onto the floor.

'Oh no!' said her teacher, feeling a bit sick and taking a deep breath. 'Let's get the caretaker to clean this up. Who could do such a thing?' (But everyone knew who!)

'Everyone, go outside, go on! Everyone *out!*' she commanded.

Imogen and Felicity couldn't eat their lunch either now. It didn't put most of the other children off though, even though they thought it was disgusting and funny. Once Rose had calmed down, she was offered a school meal, which she couldn't eat. She went outside to find Grace, Aimee, Imogen, Felicity and Jobe waiting for her.

'Do you know who did that?' they asked her.

'I have a good idea, but I can't prove it.'

'Well, I think I can,' Felicity said. 'At break time I was out late because I needed the loo, and I saw Billy by your lunchbox. Well, he was by the girls' lunchboxes anyway. He had something in his hands, a jar or tin of something, and he hid it when he saw me. I bet if the teacher searched his bag she would find it in there. There might even be some maggots left in it.'

'Right, that does it,' said Rose angrily, as the little band of friends marched back into school and knocked on the staffroom door.

Mrs. Featherspoon had been briefed on the incident. She now opened the door to the staffroom and invited the children in.

'Are you alright, Rose?' she asked. 'What happened was horrible and I will get to the bottom of this, I can assure you. Now, how can I help you?'

'Well, Miss, I think I know who did this,' said Rose. 'Felicity, tell Miss what you saw.'

'Miss, at first break I was late out because I needed the loo. I saw Billy Boot by the girls' coats and lunchboxes and he had something in his hands. If you look in Billy's school bag you might find something like a tin or jar or something.'

'Yes, Miss,' said Rose nodding.

'OK... slow down, girls.'

Mrs. Featherspoon came out of the staffroom and closed the door behind her. The children followed her to the cloakroom.

'It was Billy who threw my P.E. bag on the roof, not me, as the caretaker said,' added Jobe, as he caught them up.

'Yes, Miss, Jobe's telling the truth. I was there and saw him do it,' said Rose.

'I will deal with the P.E. bag and the detention later, Jobe. First things first.'

By now they had reached the cloakroom.

'Grace, will you go and ask Billy Boot to come here, please? Don't tell him anything. Just that Mrs. Featherspoon wants to see him in the cloakroom.'

'Yes, Miss.'

Grace soon returned with Billy and when he saw Rose and Jobe with Mrs. Featherspoon, he started to look uncomfortable.

'Billy, do you know anything about the incident with Rose's lunchbox?'

'No, Miss.'

'Can you get me your school bag, Billy, please?'

Billy took his bag off the hook and handed it to the headmistress.

'Now, Billy, it has to come to my attention that you might know something about the maggots in Rose's lunch box.'

'No, Miss.'

'Well, can I look inside your school bag?'

Billy knew he didn't have much of a choice and nodded in silence.

Mrs. Featherspoon proceeded to unzip Billy's school bag. There was a jam jar inside it, but the jar was empty.

'See?' said Billy, taking a deep sigh of relief.

Rose and Felicity looked at each other.

'Wait!' cried Grace. 'Miss, can you get his pencil case out? I saw something move.'

Mrs. Featherspoon took out Billy's pencil case. Crawling on the top of it were two maggots!

'Oh, yuck!' said Grace.

Mrs. Featherspoon emptied his bag on the floor; there were several squirming maggots wriggling around. 'Billy, what have you got to say about this?' She sounded very cross now and her voice was loud and slow.

'I don't know how they got there...' Billy started to go red.

'Billy, I don't believe you. I will ask again and I want the truth! Did you put the maggots into Rose's lunchbox?'

'Yes, Miss. Sorry, Miss,' he said quietly.

'You need to apologise to Rose, don't you?'

'Yes!' he said.

'Well?'

'Sorry, Rose.'

Mrs. Featherspoon told the children to go out and play while Billy stayed with her.

'Billy, this is serious and I will need to speak to your father before I decide what I'm going to do with you. Do you understand?'

'Yes, Miss.'

'Come with me. And Billy, what about the P.E. bag? Did you have anything to do with that?'

'Yes, a little bit.'

'What am I going to do with you, Billy? This is not good, is it? I think you had better stay with me this afternoon, so you don't get into any more trouble. I will speak to Jobe. Really, Billy, this behaviour must stop!'

While everyone else was playing outside, Billy walked off with Mrs. Featherspoon into her office.

8

AS THE CHILDREN WALKED HOME FROM SCHOOL they talked about how much they hated Billy. They had so many reasons. He was so mean; he didn't even try to be nice. It seemed to them that whenever he opened his mouth, something nasty came out.

'If only he were nicer or just kept his mouth shut more often, then maybe, just maybe, we might get on,' said Rose.

'I don't think I could ever like him,' said Jobe.

Their fathers were good friends, both being fishermen. Billy's dad, Jack, would say, 'Boys will be boys; they need to work it out between themselves, but it's a shame that they can't get on. Hopefully, someday it will change.' Dad knew that since the death of Billy's mum three years ago, Billy had become an angry boy. Nothing seemed to help.

As the children walked on, they tried to work out why Billy picked on them, especially Jobe.

'I think he must be jealous of me. I don't know why; my life's not perfect,' said Jobe.

'That's because *you're* not,' laughed Rose.

'You know, I think we should try even harder to like him, even if he is horrible,' said Grace. 'That's what the Bible says – to love our enemies.' There was a pause. 'Mmm… I'm not saying we can *love* him,' Grace added, 'but we can try and *like* him first.'

'That's impossible! I don't even *like* him. He's a selfish bully and I wouldn't trust him as far as I could throw him – and that wouldn't be very far. I don't want anything to do with him,' said Jobe.

'Grace is right.' There was a thoughtful pause after Rose spoke. 'We are supposed to forgive, even if we don't want to. It doesn't mean he's right or even what he does doesn't hurt, because most of the time it does,' she added thoughtfully.

'That's so hard. I don't know how to start liking him. In fact, I think I *hate* him.'

'Jobe, that's why we pray and ask Jesus to help us to change our feelings about him. If we don't forgive others, God will not forgive us. It says that in the Lord's Prayer, doesn't it?'

'How does it go?' Grace thought for a moment. 'Forgive us our sins as we forgive those that sin against us.' She was rather pleased with herself for remembering it.

'Yes, that's right. Do what's right, then the feelings will follow, hopefully – that's what Mum says. Anyway, we can only do our best. Jesus will have to do the rest,' said Rose.

Jobe cut in, a little frustrated that Grace and Rose were trying to act so perfect.

'Well, Jesus will *have to.* I can't do more than my best and that's going to be hard enough with Billy.'

'Let's pray for Billy tonight and see if it makes a difference,' suggested Rose.

'Rose, I don't think one night is going to make *any* difference.'

'No, you're right. OK, OK. Let's do it for a week then,' she laughed.

'What a weird thought – praying for Billy. Alright, I'll have a go,' Jobe conceded.

Jobe felt surprised and uncomfortable with what he had just agreed to do and so did his sisters, but at least they were *all* going to try praying for him, so it didn't feel completely odd and strange.

Once the children reached home, they told Mum about their horrible day and what they had decided to do with Billy.

'I am really proud of you all. Billy did some awful things today, but taking your troubles to Jesus and praying for Billy is just what Jesus wants you to do. If you want me to help you tonight, I will,' said Mum as she prepared supper. 'But I will have to tell Dad about this.'

When Dad came home, the children told him about the maggots in Rose's lunchbox, the spitting water over Jobe, the P.E. bag on the roof and the caretaker not believing them.

'I will have to speak to Jack about this; that boy's gone too far this time.' Dad was cross, and he reached for his jacket to go out again.

'Dad, wait! We are all going to pray for Billy and ask Jesus to help us with him,' said Rose. 'It's going to be an experiment.'

Dad relented. 'OK, let's "turn the other cheek" this time. But Mum and I are going in to see Mrs. Featherspoon tomorrow to see if there is something that the school can do to keep a closer eye on Billy. He needs help.'

The next morning, on arriving at school, Billy handed Rose a note.

Rose opened it. It read:

Dear Rose,

Sorry for the maggots in your lunchbox. I won't do that again. I told Mrs. Featherspoon that it was me who threw Jobe's P.E. bag on the roof. I am going to do his detention as well as mine.

Billy.

'Look,' said Rose, 'that's strange. He's never admitted or apologised before without being forced to.'

'Maybe his dad made him do it after Miss told him what he'd done,' said Jobe.

'Or maybe our prayers are working,' said Grace.

School was great. Aimee and Grace played hop-scotch during their first break and did skipping all through the lunch break. Both girls were fiercely competitive. Felicity, Imogen and Rose sat and chattered through both breaks, while Jobe, Josh and Boaz kept checking where Billy was before they joined in with the games their friends were playing. Fridays always seemed more fun.

Tomorrow was going to be different though. It was the picnic boat trip where their mum and dad would meet Skimmer, hopefully!

It read, "Dear Rose…"

9

IT WAS SATURDAY MORNING AND THE CHILDREN were up early and dressed. They felt excited and scared at the same time. Rose couldn't eat breakfast, but Jobe and Grace did. After breakfast the whole family, including Laddie, headed down to the harbour with Mum's special picnic. It felt unexpectedly good sharing their secret with their parents now everything had calmed down; now they could talk about Skimmer openly. Jobe ran on ahead, collecting a bag of small, smooth stones to skim with. Rose helped Mum carry the picnic things, while Grace was telling Dad how special Skimmer was. Laddie sniffed and peed everywhere.

Out on the boat, the sea was calm except for some small waves lapping the sides of *Miss Daisy*. Dad skilfully steered the boat out of the harbour, over to Hermit Point, and dropped anchor.

'OK, Jobe, over to you, son. See if you can call Skimmer.'

Mum and Dad watched with interest as their three children reached into Jobe's bag of stones and started skimming. There was tension in the air. This time they were out on *Miss Daisy* and it was not the same; skimming

Elaine Jenkins

stones from the boat was a lot harder. Would Skimmer come? They waited.

It didn't take too long before the familiar tail-splash caught their eye and a snout appeared.

'He's here! He's here,' the children shouted.

Skimmer jumped clean out of the water, then dived down into the cold, green sea. He swam around the boat with such speed and ease. The family was transfixed.

'Oh, he's beautiful!' Mum cried, turning to Dad. 'Look at him; he's so friendly and tame.'

Dad was quiet and just kept watching him. Skimmer had done the children's work for them: Mum was enchanted by him; Dad was impressed even if he didn't say anything; even Laddie stopped barking after a few sightings and just ran up and down the boat wagging his tail and trying to keep up with the sightings. Skimmer was so trusting, and Dad knew something needed to be done – and soon. The Evans family had all been won over by him.

Mum set the picnic out on the deck and they had the best time eating the delicious food and watching beautiful Skimmer really close up. By the time the picnic was finished, it was already late afternoon and time to make their way back into the harbour and home again.

It was after supper at the table when the conversation about Skimmer really started.

'Well, what's the plan? How are we going to save Skimmer?' Jobe asked.

Rose, who had been sitting and quietly thinking, spoke up. 'Mum, can we contact the RSPCA to come and save him? Or Marine Rescue; could they do something?'

Skimmer swam around the boat with such speed and ease.

'Good idea, love, but he's not being mistreated and he's not sick.'

'He will be if he's caught.'

'True,' Mum agreed.

'There must be something we can do. You've seen what he's like. He's so friendly; we have to take care of him and stop anyone hurting him.'

'I know, love. Rose, let's go to the library after church tomorrow and find out who it is we should contact.' Mum sounded a little concerned. 'Let's not get our hopes up. He might be caught before anything can be done.'

'We have to at least try,' replied Jobe.

'Yes, we do!' Dad said, patting Jobe on the back. 'It's just a matter of time before someone takes advantage of his gentle nature and takes things into their own hands. It's not going to be easy. Time is not on our side, so we need to work quickly and together as a team. This must be kept quiet and stay just between us for now. I wish you had told us earlier. I'm surprised that I hadn't seen him before today – and that none of the other boys have.'

'I wish we had said something sooner,' said Grace, tearing up. 'We should have told you, but we wanted to keep him our secret and we were scared of what you would do.'

Rose realised that trusting was better than keeping Skimmer a secret, which had left her feeling very miserable. This was the first time that the family had a shared secret all together, and Skimmer was depending on them.

The next day was Sunday and the Evans family went to church as usual. This time the service was about trusting God. Pastor Parker talked about when life gets hard and you don't know what to do or how to make things better. 'You must trust God,' he said. 'He has a plan and a purpose for each of us. Sometimes in life we will all go through hard, difficult and sad times. God knows us; we can trust him to work things out through us and for us. But first we have to tell him about the mess we got ourselves into and ask him for help. Then we have to trust that he will find a way to sort it out, whatever the mess, because God is God and that's what God does. He sorts our mess out. He makes it better, but different.'

Or, as Grace summed it up later, 'Do your best and God will help you with all the rest – because he loves us.'

Grace had a direct approach to life; she managed to cut through the excuses and get straight to the point. Rose could be the same, but she had a softer way of going about things, whilst Jobe could see the right way but often struggled with it. Normally he went his own way first, only asking God to help as a last resort. All three knew that Jesus died for them on the Cross; that his love was unconditional, no matter how they behaved or what came out of their mouths. They knew Jesus never gives up on those he loves, and that God loved Billy just as much as he loved each one of them. That's how special God's love is – he loves *everyone*.

Elaine Jenkins

10

THE TASK SEEMED DAUNTING, TIME WAS NOT ON
their side, but they were ready to do their best to try to save
Skimmer. Sunday lunch was a quick one; Mum made sandwiches. By two o'clock the Evans family were in the public
library, each with a job to do. It wouldn't be long before
the whole village would know about Skimmer the dolphin
and they needed to make sure he would be safe and free to
swim and go wherever he wanted. Grace and Rose had to
find a book on dolphins to find out what type Skimmer was
and how long dolphins live, what they eat, their family
groups and habits. Jobe and Dad's task was to find out the
right organisation to contact and who had the authority to
protect and save Skimmer. Then they needed to make sure
they had the support of the local newspaper, the regional
TV network and their local MP, Mr. Kenneth Pickles. It
was going to be a busy time. They had just finished collecting all the information as the library was closing.

'Now,' said Dad, 'the real work begins.'

Over the next few days, Mum sent out letters to all the
various interested parties and made several phone calls.
Before the week was out, contact had been made with the
local TV station and newspaper, *The Havenston Post*. It
seemed that they were all keen to see Skimmer.

A week later, Mr. Kenneth Pickles MP replied to his letter by post. Laddie was the first to get the post; he loved collecting the mail. As soon as he heard the clanking sound of the letterbox flap, he was there. He would collect the letters in his mouth and take them to either Dad or Mum and drop them at their feet. This morning was no different. Dad reached down to take the letters from Laddie and went through them. There was an official-looking one amongst them, so he put the rest of the mail to one side. The children had stopped eating breakfast and were watching.

'Dad, open it!' Grace said excitedly, running over to him.

'OK, OK,' he laughed. He waved the letter at her, as though he was shooing flies. 'Give me some space.'

He read the letter, then handed it over to Mum, who had just finished washing her hands and was drying them on her apron.

'Mum, what does it say? Are they going to help us save Skimmer?'

Mum gave a broad smile and said, 'Yes! It's from Kenneth Pickles. He thinks Skimmer will bring some local colour to the village and might even boost the summer tourism. He says he is coming to see us at the end of the month and wants us to arrange a date to see us.'

'Dad, that's brilliant! That gives us two weeks,' said Rose.

Grace clapped her hands and jumped up and down, while Jobe was trying to look cool and not get too excited. He didn't fool anyone though as he grinned from ear to ear.

'Yes, you three, it *is* great! Now, if we can arrange for the TV station and a reporter from the local newspaper to come out with Mr. Pickles, then we will give Skimmer a

Laddie would collect the letters in his mouth.

very public debut in front of the whole village. If Mum can get everyone to agree to come on the same day, that would be great.'

'No pressure then? Well, I'll try my best!' said Mum.

'But first we must get Skimmer tagged, so we have to hurry and book the Marine Wildlife Trust first, then he will be legally protected. Protecting Skimmer is our first priority before we tell the whole world,' said Dad.

The next week, the children didn't walk along the beach. It was hard as they missed their aquatic friend, but they didn't want to risk Skimmer being spotted. So they walked the town way home, down the high street, just to be on the safe side. It wasn't easy as it took real self-discipline, particularly from Jobe.

'You know,' Rose started, 'Mum and Dad are always telling us that a problem shared is a problem halved. I've never understood what they meant until now. With us all working together on this, it takes most of the fear away and it gives us a real chance to save Skimmer.'

True to her word, Mum had arranged all the appointments when the children returned from school. Mum called them into the kitchen for a drink and some freshly made flapjacks.

'Thanks, Mum,' said Rose. They were her favourites, and Mum made famously good, gooey flapjacks.

Mum watched with pride as her three beautiful children tucked into the treats. 'I've spoken to the Marine Wildlife Trust today. They said Dr. Butterworth and his team feel he might need protecting as he seems to be on his own and is so friendly. They even thought they would see if there is a dolphin pod nearby. They have agreed to come down this Friday to see for themselves, so it looks like you three will be having a day off school.'

Before Mum could continue, Rose choked on her juice.

'That's brilliant!' shouted Jobe, as he leaned over to Rose and gave her a rather hard slap on the back.

'Gently, Jobe... Are you alright Rose?'

Rose took a slow drink whilst nodding at her mum.

'I know it's exciting. I will need to speak to Mrs. Featherspoon. She's going to need to know why all three of you are off school, so I will have to tell her about Skimmer.'

Mrs. Featherspoon, as well as being their head teacher, was also Brown Owl for Grace's Brownie pack. Grace was certain that they would be given the day off. After all, it *was* educational; she might even get her animal badge for it.

Wednesday was a boring day that just seemed to drag on and on and on. They couldn't wait for school to finish; they just wanted to go home to catch up on any news. Mum had received another phone call from Dr. Butterworth, the head of the marine team, saying that they would be arriving at seven o'clock on Friday morning. It was early, but as the tide was high and they didn't know how long it would take to catch and tag Skimmer, this would give them the full day. They also wanted to miss the rush hour traffic.

That evening, over the supper table, the house was full of noise and getting to bed on time just didn't happen as they were all just too excited. No one could wait until Friday.

11

THURSDAY WAS INTERESTING. BILLY SPENT MOST of his lunchtime following Jobe around, picking on him again!

'When will he ever learn and when will this bullying stop?' thought Jobe.

Whenever Billy got close enough, he would give Jobe a sly push or tackle him, or just try to trip him up again. Then he would start shouting at him. 'Freckle face! You missed again! Rust bucket! What a loser!'

By now Jobe's friends were getting annoyed with Billy too.

'Go on, Jobe, sort him out. He deserves it,' Boaz urged him.

'I know he does,' said Jobe. He stopped playing football and walked over to Billy.

The game stopped. Jobe's friends watched to see how the drama would unfold.

'Billy, if you want to play, you just have to ask,' Jobe said, then smiled at him and walked off, leaving Billy standing there in front of Jobe's friends, who were just as surprised by what had just happened. They had been secretly hoping for a fight.

Jobe felt pleased with himself. Normally, when Billy got too much, he would punch him a couple of times, a fight would begin, and they would both end up in detention outside Mrs. Featherspoon's office after school. This time he had controlled his fists *and* his mouth. This was massive progress.

Five minutes later the bell went for end of break.

'Maybe praying for Billy is working,' thought Jobe, 'but it's me who's become kinder and more self-controlled, not him. That's strange…'

At the end of school, Jobe and Grace were out by the school gates waiting for Rose, who was late.

'Sorry, Felicity wanted to tell me about her birthday present. She's got tickets for our favourite band and she's asked me and Imogen to go with her. I can't believe it. It's next month and we get to go backstage and meet them. Wait till I tell Mum. Of course, I'll stay at hers for a sleepover because it's going to be such a late night. I can't wait.'

'Yeah, well, Grace and I have been waiting ages for you,' Jobe grumbled.

Rose ignored him. Nothing he said was going to ruin her news. This would be her *first ever concert!* And she was going with her best friends to see her favourite band. Life just didn't get any better than this…

That evening after supper they all prepared for an early start as Dr. Butterworth and his team would be arriving early. There were waterproofs to get out and packed lunches to prepare. The alarm clock had to be set so they would be up in time, then everyone needed to have a bath and wash their hair. Grace was helping Mum in the kitchen. She liked cooking and it was also her way of making sure there were a few favourites packed in the picnic. The children would sometimes play on their parents' phones in the evening, but not tonight. No one was staring at the TV, and nobody was interested in the Play-Station or the Wii. They were all enjoying being together and talking about what could happen tomorrow. Finally, everything was ready.

Rose, Jobe and Grace went up to bed, but it was impossible to sleep, so the girls snuck out of bed and went into Jobe's room. There they sat on his bed and played cards in a whisper.

It wasn't long though before Mum shouted up the stairs. 'Get to bed you three or you won't be going any-where tomorrow. You will be staying home and that's a promise.'

'Mum, we can't sleep,' protested Rose.

'Well, you all have a book you're reading. You may read for ten minutes in your own rooms, then I'll be up to turn the lights out – *again,* but this better be the last time.'

Tonight was not the night to push it, so Rose and Grace went back to their own rooms and Jobe tidied up his cards and got his favourite comic out.

Shortly after seven o'clock the next morning, there was a knock on the door. The family hadn't heard it, but Laddie had. He started to bark and bark, until he woke up the whole house.

'Oh, no!' shrieked Mum. 'They're here. Look at me!' She grabbed her dressing gown, slipped her slippers on and ran downstairs to open the front door. She smoothed out her hair with her hands, as she didn't want the bedhead

*The children sat on Jobe's bed and
played cards in a whisper.*

look when she opened the front door, especially as it was the first time she was meeting the team.

Dad called out to the children, but they were already getting dressed.

'I'm so sorry, I don't know what happened, my alarm didn't wake me up. Please, come in.' Still smoothing down her hair with her hands, Mum ushered Dr. Butterworth and his team into the lounge, then she went to the kitchen to put the kettle on.

Dad was soon downstairs dressed and ready to take over from Mum. After he'd introduced himself, Mum slipped past him and whispered, 'What happened to the alarm? Tea's made; it's in the kitchen.'

There were four people in Dr. Butterworth's team. The youngest in the team was Rueben, a university graduate who looked like a surfer rather than a researcher. The second, Malcolm, had white, wispy hair and bright blue eyes; he was in charge of all the technical equipment. The only woman in the team was Faith; she was slim and pretty with long blonde hair, which she wore in plaits. Faith assisted Malcolm and Dr. Butterworth. The final team member was Dr. Butterworth himself, who was in charge and introduced himself as Thomas. He was in his forties, tall with brown hair and a dark suntan.

The rush and hectic start was a great icebreaker. Now the house was full of chatter and noise. Once they were all up and dressed, Thomas and his team finished their tea. No one wanted any breakfast, so they were soon heading out of the cottage towards the harbour.

They passed a few school friends. 'Rose,' one of them called out, 'why aren't you going to school? What's going on? Where are you going?'

Rose shouted back as she rushed past. 'I'll tell you later. Miss knows all about this, don't worry. I'll see you in church on Sunday or maybe at school on Monday.'

Billy Boot had watched as the four strangers and all the Evans family had gone past carrying a long, heavy bag and a picnic hamper. He wanted to know what was going on, so he hung back and followed them down to the harbour. He watched as they got into the fishing boat *Miss Daisy* and pulled out onto the waves.

Suddenly a car horn blasted right next to him. Billy jumped out of his skin. It was Jack, Billy's dad, in his Land Rover. 'Billy,' he yelled in a cross voice, 'get in!' The passenger door flung open and Billy got into the car, his father's voice ringing in his ears as he drove him straight to school.

At the morning assembly, the headmistress announced to the school that the Evans children had found a lone dolphin and that the Marine Wildlife Trust team were down to catalogue and tag him. The children were needed to show where the dolphin was likely to be. There was an excited wave of whispers as the children talked to each other about how lucky Rose, Jobe and Grace were, not only finding the dolphin, but missing a day off school. But Billy was feeling resentful and jealous. Why was it that family again? Why should they have all the fun? Why was everyone else so pleased for them? Why did they have so many friends? It just wasn't fair. Billy found Grace really irritating, mouthy and stubborn. He thought Rose was arrogant and always tried to act like she knew everything.

Skimmer

Jobe – well, he was the biggest pain of them all. Billy just hated him.

12

OUT ON THE BOAT, SKIMMER HAD BEEN SPOTTED and they didn't even need to use their stones to call him over this time. The team got busy getting ready. Dr. Butterworth told them that it was a young bottlenose dolphin (which they already knew from their library research), approximately three years old, and that it must have somehow got lost from its family group.

Rueben, dressed in his wetsuit, fins, snorkel and mask, fell backwards off the boat into the sea, staying close to the side of the vessel. He was ready to secure the net when it was thrown over Skimmer, to see that the dolphin didn't get too tangled up in the process. Skimmer came in close, not expecting to be trapped. Then, once he was close enough, the net was thrown over him. It was horrible! Poor, trusting Skimmer panicked. He didn't know what was happening. He thrashed his tail and tried to dive down out of the net, but the more he struggled, the more he got caught up. Rueben swam around him, checking on him, then gave the signal to lift him up out of the water. Skimmer seemed terrified.

'Oh, Mum, it's horrible. He's not going to die, is he?' cried Rose. Grace pulled Dr. Butterworth's arm and yelled at him. 'You're hurting him. *Let him go!*' she shouted. Then she gave him two hard kicks in the shin.

'Ow!' he said, bending down to rub his shin.

Rueben, dressed in his wetsuit, fins, snorkel and mask, fell backwards off the boat into the sea.

'Grace!' Mum said in a stern tone. 'Sorry, Thomas, she sometimes lashes out when she gets really angry. Grace, I know this doesn't look very nice, but Dr. Butterworth knows what he is doing. If we stay calm and out of their way, they can do their job quickly and then they can release Skimmer. Come here with me.' She took Grace by the hand and away from the main action.

Grace stood in front of her, so she could still see what was going on. Mum had her arms around her youngest to comfort her and hold her back in case Grace felt the need to lash out again. It seemed like such a long struggle, but finally Skimmer was pulled onto the boat. Then the team got busy, weighing, measuring and tagging him. Grace ran to Skimmer and was stroking his head and talking quietly to him. Her voice seemed to calm him. He didn't fight and thrash as much; he lay still and motionless, apart from his eyes which blinked at Grace as she talked to him. She knew Skimmer was trusting her with his life.

Grace had never felt anything like this before. She watched as the team skilfully ran through their tests, one by one. 'Can you hurry up? He's so scared and he wants to get back in the sea,' she said anxiously.

'Just one minute. We need to take some of his blood, then we're done.' Dr. Butterworth got out the syringe with the thickest, longest needle Grace had ever seen.

'No, stop! You can't do that,' Grace yelled at him again, putting herself in the way of Skimmer, who had now started to thrash his tail about, trying to swish himself free.

'Grace, his blood will tell us if he is healthy or carrying any parasites that could affect not just him but any other dolphin pod in the area. It's so important we do this. He'll feel a scratch, just like you would at the doctor's, but I promise I will be as quick and as gentle as I can. Then we will lower Skimmer back into the sea. *I promise,*' said Dr. Butterworth. He looked straight at Grace. He could see her eyes were filling up although she was trying not to cry. 'It's all OK. We need to do this but then it will all be finished and you and your brother and sister can help me put him back in the sea.' Dr. Butterworth spoke both firmly and calmly.

Grace nodded and moved aside, allowing Dr. Butterworth to inject Skimmer and take a sample of his blood. It was only after he had finished that Rose and Jobe got their chance to touch him. He was smooth, almost silky, but the biggest surprise was that he was warm.

It was now that Mum whispered to Grace. 'Darling, I think you need to apologise to Dr. Butterworth, don't you?'

Grace gave her a half-turn and quick nod. She got up and went over to Dr. Butterworth and pulled his sleeve. He stopped working and looked at her. 'Sorry for kicking you, I shouldn't have,' she said in her very matter-of-fact way.

'That's alright, I'll live. Now, we have to get this little fella back into the sea. Do you want to help me?'

'Oh, yes please!'

The children gave Skimmer a final kiss. Rose took her camera out and took as many pictures as she could as they helped the team gently lower him over the side of the boat in a marine sling. Within moments of the water immersing him, Skimmer was gone.

'Well done, everyone, good work,' Dr. Butterworth said. 'We will take these results back to the institute and add them to our data. He's a fine specimen. It's good to see bottlenose dolphins coming back into these waters; their numbers seem to be increasing. Even if we haven't found this young fella's family pod yet, they can't be far away.'

After the picnic was finished, it was time for *Miss Daisy* and all aboard to return to the harbour. By now it was late afternoon. The Evans family waved goodbye to Dr. Butterworth and his team. The day had been a real adventure, one they would never forget. But the best bit was that Skimmer was now protected and would be monitored for the rest of his life. They knew now that he was a male dolphin and how much he weighed and roughly how old he was.

Dad hung up the waterproofs, and the children kicked off their wellies, flopped onto the sofa and flicked the TV on. Mum had gone into the kitchen to fix the evening meal and Laddie had followed, barking for his own supper.

'What a day,' yawned Rose. 'I'll sleep well tonight.'

'Me too,' agreed Jobe, yawning after her.

The next week flew by and the children had so many questions to answer about Skimmer at school. The dolphin was famous. Mum had also successfully managed to arrange for the TV crew and a reporter from the town newspaper to come out with Mr. Kenneth Pickles on *Miss Daisy* to see him.

13

DAD HAD TOLD HIS CHILDREN THAT THERE WAS not going to be enough room for all three of them to come out on the boat with the TV crew, local reporter and MP Mr. Pickles, but he had come up with a plan.

'I know you all want to come out, but I can only take one of you on the boat this time. There just isn't room with all the equipment and it won't be safe. So, to make it fair, you can each pick matchsticks to see which one of you will get to come. Whoever gets the *longest* one can join us. Wait here; I will get three matches.'

He turned and walked into the kitchen, where he found the matchbox and took out three matches and broke two in half. Then he put them in his hand so that only the heads were sticking out. Dad came back into the lounge.

'Now,' he said in his serious voice, 'the person with the longest match is coming on the boat with me and that's an end to it. No arguments and no discussion. OK?'

Rose, Jobe and Grace looked at each other and nodded.

'Grace, as you are the youngest, would you like to go first?'

'Yes please!' She looked carefully at the matches trying to get a clue of which was the longest but couldn't. Finally, she pulled out a short one.

'Oh, that's not fair!' she moaned.

'Rose, it's your turn.'

'Why is it Rose's turn? I'm the next youngest,' complained Jobe.

'Maybe so, but ladies first, Jobe; that's just good manners.'

'Thanks!' smiled Rose. Then she looked at the two matches left. 'Um... I don't know which one to choose.' After a moment or two she pulled one out – but it was a short match. 'Oh, well, we will see Skimmer again, won't we?' She tried not to sound too disappointed.

'Of course you will,' smiled Dad.

Jobe didn't need to draw a match. 'That means I've won!' he said. 'Brilliant!' He couldn't help beaming in sheer delight. 'It looks like it's Dad and me then,' he said feeling very excited.

'It looks like it, son.' Dad placed a hand on Jobe's shoulder.

The girls were disappointed, but they knew it was fair. 'Well done, Jobe. I wish it was me going,' smiled Rose as Grace stormed off into the kitchen.

On Saturday morning, the reporter from *The Havenston Post* and the local TV crew arrived at the house shortly after nine o'clock. Mr. Kenneth Pickles was running a little late. He eventually arrived though, and they then set off down to the harbour to find Dad's boat, *Miss Daisy*. Mum and the girls waved the party off from the harbour. By now the whole village knew about Skimmer and there was a large crowd gathering.

There was quite a strong breeze and the sea was choppy. A few other fishermen and their families were waiting at the harbour. The news had spread throughout the town about Havenston's dolphin and most of the fishermen, along with their families, were waiting to follow *Miss Daisy* over to Hermit Point.

Jack Boot and Billy were amongst them. Billy was not a good swimmer, he didn't like water much, and the rare times he did go out with his dad, he was often seasick. To Billy, Skimmer was just a stupid big fish, like any other; free to be caught by anyone who could catch him. Billy wanted to catch him so badly and kill him, mostly to hurt Jobe and to steal the limelight. *Who has ever heard of a pet dolphin anyway?*

A flotilla of little boats sailed out of the harbour behind *Miss Daisy.* When they arrived, Dad threw the anchor out of the boat, to the right of Hermit Point. The other boats did the same, forming a horseshoe shape, lining up on either side of *Miss Daisy.* Everyone watched as Jobe took out his smooth stones and started to skim them across the water.

It took a while before the familiar tail splash was spotted. Skimmer swam straight towards Jobe, but not too close this time. He kept his distance. It made it easier for everyone on their boats to see him as well, and people were taking photos and filming him on their smartphones. The TV crew started to film. It was a lovely sight; the children and families on the other boats started to cheer Skimmer, who loved it and played up to all the attention.

Jack had anchored near to Miss Daisy, so Billy was close to all the action. Skimmer dived down and jumped up, making his wonderful half-moon shapes. He smacked his tail on the water, soaking those closest and making them shriek with laughter. Skimmer made his happy clicks and whistle noises, which delighted the floating crowd.

Meanwhile, no one was watching Billy. He had gone into his father's fishing box and got out one of the fishing nets. Jack, like the others, hadn't noticed what Billy was up to, as Billy shoved as much of the net as he could up his jumper. But there was so much of it, it dangled all around him.

Billy was moving closer to the side of the boat, getting ready to catch Skimmer. He didn't notice that his father's oilskin coat had fallen out of the fishing box and onto the deck. The choppy water rocked the boats from side to side, and then a big wave came and tilted them even more. Billy tried to steady himself, but he stepped onto the oilskin coat and slid right over to the side of the boat. The net was falling out of his jumper as he grabbed the side of the boat, then a split second later another wave came. He lost his balance and within seconds he had toppled overboard! The net had poured out from under his jumper and had wrapped around him.

Billy splashed and screamed, alerting everyone to what had just happened. Jack raced down to the side where he had fallen in and tried to grab him, but he was too far down in the water and kept sinking. When he did come up, Jack couldn't reach him; his screaming and his thrashing around just made it worse. The rocking of the waves didn't help either and the net tightened around him so that his arms became entangled within it. He couldn't move; he couldn't swim; he couldn't stay up. All the while he was drifting away from his father's boat.

Jack had never been so scared in his life. He threw Billy a rope, but Billy couldn't use his arms and hands as they were too tightly tangled. So he threw Billy a life ring which

Billy splashed and screamed, alerting everyone to what had just happened.

landed close to him. 'Grab it, son,' he shouted, but Billy could only move his fingers.

Billy's screams could be heard everywhere. He tried to free himself and grab the ring, but couldn't; he was caught up in the very net he had been trying to catch Skimmer in. He was panicking and when he screamed he took in mouthfuls of seawater. He was getting weaker and weaker, drifting farther away from his father's boat. Jack had taken off his jacket and jumper and was about to dive into the cold sea to save his terrified son... when it happened.

Skimmer swam underneath him and gently lifted him up, so that Billy could catch his breath. The dolphin stayed under him, stopping him from sinking.

Billy grabbed Skimmer's dorsal fin with his bound-up hands and leant over him as if to ride him. Everyone just stared; they couldn't believe what they were seeing. Jobe then started to call Skimmer.

'Skimmer, over here! Come on, that's it! Good dolphin! Keep coming!'

Skimmer swam over to Miss Daisy, slowly bringing a terrified Billy with him. Jobe leaned over as far as he dared and within seconds Billy was next to Jobe and within reach. Jobe grabbed him by the back of his jumper and held on as tight as he could. It wasn't easy, as Billy was heavy, wet and very scared. The waves didn't help and the rocking of the boat made it all the more difficult, but Jobe wasn't going to give up.

'Quick, Dad! Help me!'

Dad was right there by Jobe's side and as the two of them pulled a frightened, sobbing, soaking Billy onboard, Skimmer darted away.

'Jack, we have him!' Dad yelled. 'He's OK! He's OK, mate. We've got him.'

14

JOBE STARTED CUTTING AWAY AT THE NET WITH Dad's Swiss army knife. Dad fetched a blanket from the cabin and put it around Billy.

'It's alright son, you're safe now,' he said, giving the boy a rub down. Billy coughed and spluttered, shaking with cold and fear.

Jobe gave Billy a mug of hot chocolate, but Billy was shaking too much to hold it.

'Billy, are you alright? Billy? That was a close call.'

Billy just sat there shivering and sobbing; he had never been so scared. He had just been rescued by the dolphin he had been trying to catch and kill. Then to be pulled to safety by the boy he hated... How bad could it get? Billy had all these mixed feelings flooding in on him, as tears poured down his face.

'You're OK now, Billy,' said Jobe, looking at him. 'I see you've met Skimmer. What do you think?' He was trying to lighten the mood as he handed a snotty Billy a tissue.

'I nearly drowned. I *would* have done, if it wasn't for you and your dolphin.' Billy started to sob again. 'I've been such an idiot.'

Jobe leaned closer to his enemy, blocking the film crew's view. 'You weren't trying to catch him, were you, Billy?' he whispered.

'Billy, are you alright? Billy?' Jobe said.

'I'm so sorry,' Billy whimpered. 'It's worse than you think. I wanted to catch him and... I might have hurt him and...'

But Jobe interrupted. 'It's OK. It's really OK. We *all* mess up sometimes. You aren't planning to hurt him now, are you?' he added half-jokingly.

Billy couldn't speak; tears kept coming as he shook his head and choked out, 'No! How could I?'

'That's a relief!' Jobe put his arm around Billy, something he had never done before.

Back on the boat, the camera crew had caught the whole rescue on film. Skimmer was not just a local dolphin now, he was a local hero too. So, for that matter, was Jobe. Mr. Pickles leant over to Dad and whispered, 'What a boy, that boy of yours! He deserves a reward for such quick thinking. What a day! What a day! Wouldn't have missed it for the world.'

Once Billy was untangled and cut loose from Jack's net, he started to calm down. He was so cold, he just couldn't stop shivering, so Dad wrapped him in his coat and a dry blanket, while Jobe gave him more hot chocolate to drink.

Slowly the flotilla of fishing boats sailed back to the harbour. Once they were all safely docked, Jack couldn't wait. He jumped out of his boat and ran over to Miss Daisy, then climbed aboard and hugged a very wet, sad Billy.

'What were you thinking, boy?' he said. Then he turned to Jobe's dad. 'Thanks, mate. I can't thank you enough.' He looked at Jobe too and ruffled his hair and kissed him. 'Jobe, you saved my boy, you and that dolphin of yours. You saved Billy's life.'

Then Jack helped Billy off the boat and the two of them headed for his Land Rover.

Dad turned to Jobe. 'I am so proud of you. You did a very brave thing out there, son. Well done!' Dad hugged Jobe and kissed him on top of his head, just as Jack had done.

'You know, Dad, the first thing I thought of when I saw Billy splashing and going under was, "Oh, Lord Jesus, what should I do?" Then in my head I heard, "I died for Billy too." I suddenly knew. It was easy. I just called Skimmer over, just like I call Laddie, then leaned over the side of the boat and grabbed him as tight as I could until you came to help me pull him up. He *was* really heavy, wasn't he?'

They both laughed.

'Do you know what's strange? Billy has always been horrible to me. In fact, you know I probably hated him. You know we've never got on, but something changed out there. As soon as I saw him, I knew I had to help him. My bad feelings towards him had gone. I don't get it and I don't understand it, but it feels great. Is this what God does? Because I know it wasn't me. Who knows, we might even get to be friends – or is that pushing it?'

They both started to laugh out loud. Dad looked at his son. 'I am so proud of you! Come on, son, let's go home.'

'Dad, it's just a shame that Rose, Mum and Grace weren't here to see it. Grace won't believe it.'

'Oh, she will, don't worry! Remember, it was all caught on film.'

They both laughed with their arms around each other as they started to walk home. They knew this was one day they would never forget... and neither would Billy.

About the Author

Elaine Jenkins lives in South Wales with her husband Neil, their dog, two cats, a few hens and a horse. They have three grown-up children and, so far, three beautiful grandchildren, Imogen, Boaz and Rueben.

Elaine qualified as a Nanny, then went onto Drama School in Guildford (now part of Guildford University) where she studied for two years.

Many of Elaine's children's stories are based upon those she created for her own children when they were young; now many more children will be able to enjoy them. Her first piece of work, which she self-published in 2015, was *Daphne and the Biggest Egg in the World,* but she has always written poems and children's stories for pleasure; it is only now, more recently, that her collections have been gathered together and prepared for publishing. The first of these stories is *Skimmer.*

"Elaine Jenkins seamlessly weaves deep Christian truth into a children's story that, like Skimmer the dolphin, captures the heart. It makes you wish that you were eight again; I would have loved this story!"

Kate Patterson
Minister and Author